# THE
# THREE MEN IN A BOAT
## COMPANION
### THE THAMES OF JEROME K. JEROME

STEPHEN LAMBE

*To My Father, Ronnie, who introduced me to* Three Men in a Boat *in the first place*

## Thanks and Acknowledgements

I would like to thank the following people who generously contributed pictures and information for this book: Campbell McCutcheon, The American Library of Congress, Cygnet Rowing Club, Nancy Hood, Tim Everson, Pamela Horn, Mike Cherry, John Sheaf, Ken Howe, Ed Harris, Philip Lambe, Ronnie Lambe, Chris Walkden and my late Mother Ann Lambe. Thanks also to: Rosemary and Vivien Lambe and as always my gorgeous wife Gill.

## Literary Sources:

The annotated edition of *Three Men in a Boat* by Christopher Matthew and Benny Green, published by Pavilion in 1982, was a huge source of information. The illustrations that accompanied the first edition of *Three Men in a Boat* by A. Frederics have been liberally used. *The Michael Palin Diaries – The Python Years*. *The Thames Path* by David Sharp (Aurum) and *Maybe It's Because*, the autobiography of Hubert Gregg.

First published 2012

Amberley Publishing
The Hill, Stroud
Gloucestershire, GL5 4EP

www.amberley-books.com

British Library Cataloguing in Publication Data.
A catalogue record for this book is available from the British Library.

ISBN 978 1 4456 0778 8

Typeset in 10pt on 12pt Sabon.
Typesetting and Origination by Amberley Publishing.
Printed in the UK.

# Contents

# Three Men in a Boat

## (TO SAY NOTHING OF THE DOG)

BY

## JEROME K. JEROME

AUTHOR OF

"IDLE THOUGHTS OF AN IDLE FELLOW,"
"STAGE LAND," ETC.

## Illustrations by A. Frederics.

BRISTOL
J. W. ARROWSMITH, 11 QUAY STREET
LONDON
SIMPKIN, MARSHALL, HAMILTON, KENT & CO. LIMITED

1889

# Introduction

Talking about *Three Men in a Boat* with a colleague recently, we discussed his reluctance to read this 'classic' due to having to endure Fielding's *Tom Jones* at school. I pointed out that literary 'classics' come in many shapes and sizes, and that Jerome's comic masterpiece is about the most readable to be found in that section of any bookshop. Not that it is necessarily as 'light' as it is sometimes cracked up to be. Jerome's themes are universal – those little hypocrisies that we live with every day: how trying to impress one's peers can become obsessive beyond the point of logic; how friendship can be just as much about bickering and one-upmanship as it is about tolerance and love. Many of the anecdotes that pepper *Three Men in a Boat* ring as true today as they did when the book was written in 1889. We may not, generally speaking, sing comic songs to bemused audiences in the twenty-first century like Harris did, but we all know someone who has let his self-delusion override the logic of his circumstances. Some of us see that every week on Saturday night television! To use another famous example from the book, J's hypochondria will be familiar to us all, even if not all of the solutions suggested to him for his ailments would be recommended by twenty-first-century pharmacists: early nights and long walks, yes; the steak and bitter beer taken every 6 hours, probably not. The other universal truth is that animals – in this case Montmorency – are wiser than us most of the time, and this remains as true today as it was in 1889.

Then there is the river. Was there ever a more evocative and affectionate portrait of a waterway? *Three Men in a Boat* is not the travelogue that Jerome initially intended it to be, but there was enough of the river left in the book to help boost river tourism by 50 per cent in the year after the book was published in 1889. The boaters and colourful blazers still to be found at Henley week belong to Jerome's time and no other.

I first read *Three Men in a Boat* in my early teens, under the influence of my father. I read a great deal of literature from, or set in, the Victoria era around this time: I remember loving the Sherlock Holmes stories and McDonald-Fraser's Flashman books particularly, as well as the supernatural tales of Sheridan Le Fanu and M. R. James. But it was the humour and warmth of Jerome that brought me back to *Three Men* time and time again. That and the familiarity of his settings. My family has always had a close association with the river. My parents met at adjacent rowing clubs near Weybridge. My father, aged 16 in 1941, took his own trip up the Thames with his friends Peter and John Oakey. My immediate family spent many a happy week at our holiday home – a bungalow by the Thames near Shepperton Lock owned by the Civil Service Rowing

Weybridge from Hamhaugh Island, 24 July 2008.

Club. I was later to hold my wedding reception there, the location having the advantage of being both beautiful and cheap. So resonant was that time that my brother and sister, now in their forties, both live on the banks of the Thames to this day.

This book is both an affectionate tribute to Jerome's wonderful work and a celebration of the river itself, or at least the part that meanders from Kingston to Oxford, the extent of J, George and Harris' trip. The first part of the book discusses *Three Men in a Boat*, placing it in the context of its time and place. It is not intended to be a detailed dissection of the book, nor is it attempting to analyse the book sentence by sentence. For that, I recommend Christopher Matthew and the late Benny Green's magnificent annotated edition, published in the 1980s. Copies are still available second hand. The latter part of this book takes the reader on the journey from Kingston to Oxford as Jerome would have experienced it. In the main, I have concentrated on the same points of interest as Jerome, although it has not been possible to include every single landmark. I have, on the other hand, lingered in Henley and in Oxford itself a little longer than Jerome did, but these are such important and interesting stopping off points that a little poetic licence has been used. With some exceptions I have not strayed far from the river in my photography, and I have tried to keep the pictures varied. Beautiful though greenery is, a view of Cliveden Reach looks much the same as Culham Cut when reproduced in a book like this, so I have tried to avoid repetition where possible.

This book has few pretensions other than providing, as the title says, a modest companion to Jerome's finest work, and I hope it enhances the pleasure of reading it, whether you are doing so for the first or the hundredth time.

Stephen Lambe
July 2012

Two photographs from a trip taken by Ronnie Lambe, the author's father, in 1941, inspired by *Three Men in a Boat*. The Camping skiff he and his colleagues used was similar to the one that Jerome and companions would have used. Note the limited storage space fore and aft and the hoops that allow the canvas cover to stretch over the boat for sleeping under. Three men would not have been terribly comfortable in the 1880s or the 1940s!

# Jerome Klapka Jerome

To those for whom Jerome exemplifies the newly leisured Victorian middle classes with his comfortable bachelor's life, the reality of his origins may come as a shock. He was born the youngest of four children in Walsall in 1859. His father owned mines at Cannock Chase but moved to London on his own in 1862 following the collapse of his business, to attempt to rebuild his life in wholesale ironmongery. The family joined him soon afterwards but lurched in and out of poverty. However, Jerome did win a place at Marylebone Grammar school, which he left, somewhat disaffected with the education he had received, at the age of 14.

Jerome tried a few professions before settling on writing. He became a clerk at a ticket office at Euston Station. He used his overtime money to attend the theatre, but when his sister Blandina married and moved away, he was left to look after his ailing mother, his father having died a few years previously. When his mother died he was still only 15. Eventually, the lonely youth drifted into acting, becoming a touring player with a variety of companies. This time seemed to give him a grounding in life but failed to make him a rich man, and when he finally returned to London, he had thirty shillings in his pocket.

He tried becoming a schoolmaster before tiding himself over in secretarial jobs. But writing was his calling and after numerous attempts to break into journalism, an autobiographical piece, 'On Stage and Off – The Brief career of a Would Be Actor', was sold to a magazine called *The Play*, netting him his first, delightfully crisp, five pound note. The book was later published by the Leadenhall Press and was (as Jerome notes in *My Life and Times*) slated by the critics although it sold decently. Jerome seems to have been a victim of the critics throughout his career and his next book, *Idle Thoughts of an Idle Fellow*, fared just as badly with the critics but did even better commercially. Today, Jerome would have been a internet 'blogger'. His books are full of wry opinion, some of it useful and some of it less so, and his writing in *Idle Thoughts* has a pleasant 'throw away' quality that makes reading it today pleasurable but inconsequential – particularly because many of his insights into Victorian life have not dated at all.

And thus a career blossomed. Jerome married Ettie in 1888 and settled at the couple's first home together in Chelsea Gardens. He became a celebrated – by the public at least – author and playwright, living a largely comfortable life, although his ventures into magazine publishing were not without incident and difficulty. A sequel to *Three Men in a Boat* called *Three Men on the Bummel* attempted to re-visit the successful formula by featuring his three heroes and contained some marvellous set pieces. However, by setting the book on a cycling tour of Germany it failed to find the same resonance with the public as the earlier book, and it sold relatively modestly. He served in the First World War as an ambulance driver with the French army and published an autobiography, My *Life and Times*, in 1926. He died the following year of a stroke while on a motoring tour.

Like many people since – actors, writers and artists particularly – Jerome lived a respectable, successful professional life overshadowed by one huge success. His work might have earned himself a decent living without ever troubling posterity, but one book found a different audience almost immediately – and never lost it.

Jerome K. Jerome in later life

Three ages of Jerome. Jerome's birthplace in Walsall. The museum has now, sadly, closed. The plaque and street sign show where Jerome wrote *Three Men in a Boat* in Chelsea Gardens, just after his marriage to Ettie. Finally, Jerome's gravestone in St Mary's Church, Ewelme, in Oxfordshire.

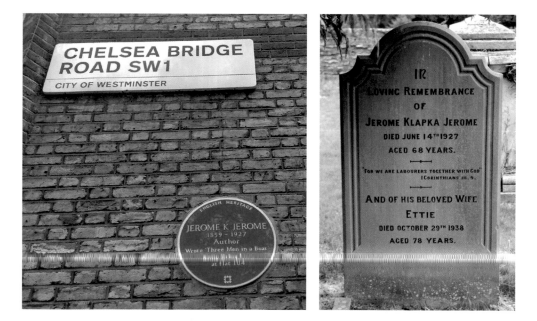

# *Three Men in a Boat* – The Book

Jerome first met bank clerk George Wingrave in London when they lodged together to save money just after Jerome stopped acting. It would appear that the optimism that George displays in *Three Men* was a genuine trait and he often encouraged Jerome in his journalistic endeavours. Jerome was also a member of a theatrical discussion group called The Old Vagabond Club where he met the other member of the party, a photographer of Polish extraction called Carl Hentschel, to be immortalised as Harris. There may have been other friends and other permutations in their trips on the Thames, but it was this perfect group of three that worked when creating his masterwork. At weekends or occasionally for longer trips, Jerome and friends would take the train to Kingston or Richmond to spend time on the river.

However, it was not a specific trip on the Thames with his friends that inspired his book, but his honeymoon with new wife Ettie in 1888. The trip they took on the river was a nostalgic one for Jerome, and he set about a book inspired by his love for the river. The book was originally to be titled *The Story of the Thames* and to be about its scenery and history with some humorous relief. Some of that book still remains, of course, and it would have been a passably interesting read, with no longevity whatsoever. Jerome decided to write the humorous relief first, to get it out of the way, and that is what seems to have remained. To some extent, we can thank one F. W. Robinson, the editor of an otherwise forgotten magazine called *Home Chimes* for the slant of the book. He removed most of Jerome's attempts at history, and to him we should be eternally grateful.

## The Anecdotes

From the very first sequence – Jerome's hilarious dissection of his own hypochondria – the book combines the trip up the river with the 'light relief' mentioned earlier. Some of these are not introduced with much subtlety. The early anecdote about Uncle Podger hanging a painting, while terrifically funny, has no bearing on the book whatsoever. These tend to be dropped in with little more than a 'that reminds me of', particularly in the early part of the book. What makes these, nonetheless, so gratifying is the way each one builds like an exceptionally sophisticated stand-up comedy routine. There is something inherently funny about cheese, admittedly, but the section in chapter four where Jerome takes a couple of cheeses home from Liverpool by train builds in hilarity until the unnamed cheeses have to be buried in sand at the seaside to keep the public safe from them.

As the book continues, and the trio finally get on the river – a third of the way into the book – the stories become more closely related to the Thames. We get Jerome's views on girls (they are all a bit silly on the whole, it would seem), on fishing (fishermen tend to exaggerate), on how awful steam launches are (really awful, unless you are being towed by one) and the perils of using a towing line ('Oh Henry, then where is auntie?'). Sometimes the stories relate directly to the current journey – particularly George's wildly optimistic stew ('so fresh and piquant'). Sometimes Jerome tells us they relate to other trips – like the incident with the photographer at Hampton Court which actually comes later in the book ('Look to your nose, can't you?'). Jerome is quite subtle about this, so that the reader, several pages on, forgets whether what they have just read relates to the current trip or not. Each incident becomes part of one glorious journey.

Jerome's derision is handed out fairly even-handedly, although there are some slightly shocking passages that jar slightly these days. Harris and J's accoster at Kempton Park is treated with snobbish contempt, and Jerome is exceptionally rude to the old man desperate to show him some tombs a few pages later. We are expected to find these sections funny, but they fall a touch flat. Elsewhere, the jokes are better judged. While Harris' pomposity gets plenty of coverage, as does George's slightly dim optimism, Jerome is just as happy sending himself up, alongside anyone else he meets. It is life's little hypocrisies that Jerome is interested in, those pompous barriers that we all put up and

'Oh Henry, then where is auntie?'

the white lies many of us tell to make us occasionally appear better than we are in front of our peers. In a sense, this is quite a cynical view of life, and some commentators have suggested that this is a flaw in the book. Most of us, however, are charmed by them.

## Jerome's flights of fancy and fantasy

Jerome, it is clear, took himself quite seriously as a writer, and fancied himself a poet. The book is littered with florid diversions. Benny Green, in his perceptive introduction to the 1982 annotated edition, rather unkindly describes *Three Men in a Boat* as one of the most skipped books in history, due to these rather ripe passages. On the basis that moderation is all things is good, I must admit I rather like them. To begin with, Jerome seems to apologise for these sentimental diversions, ending one particular evocation of the pleasures of camping out with Harris' blunt, 'How about when it rained?' Later on, these diversions are inserted without comment, the most lengthy being Jerome's speculative re-imagining of the signing of the Magna Carta.

## To say nothing of the dog ...

As Jerome reminds us in his autobiography, *My Life and Times*:

> There never was a dog. I did not possess one at that time. Neither did George. Nor did Harris ... Montmorency I evolved out of my inner consciousness. There is something of the dog, I take it, in most Englishmen. Dog friends I have come to know later tell me that he was true to life.

So, why is the dog in the book? What purpose does he serve?

Montmorency seems to represent the conscience of the three protagonists. He spots their buffoonery and their hypocrisies and he comments on them, usually with a sulk or an ironic gesture. When George creates his epic Irish stew at Shiplake, he produces a dead rat to add to the feast. Jerome comments that he is unclear whether this is a genuine contribution or a sarcastic comment on proceedings. But we know. Of course we do. He is outvoted when the first plans for a river trip are mooted; he comments robustly when George plays his banjo, and howls with sadness when George does the same thing in different circumstances later in the book. In other respects he is a normal dog, albeit the sort that likes a fight, while having an almost angelic appearance. Montmorency has a comic dislike of cats, but comes a cropper in Marlow, where the merest look from a Tom – beautifully articulated by Jerome in a 'conversation' between the two animals – traumatises the poor animal.

Montmorency is there where a comment is required, someone to wink at the reader to say, 'WE know what's going on, aren't those three men idiots?' Yet he has as strong a personality as any of the four major characters. As Benny Green so beautifully put it, Jerome's fictitious dog is 'perverse and quixotic', always contrary, and always up

Jerome's fictitious Fox Terrier, as imagined by A. Frederics.

for a battle. While *Three men in a Boat* might still have been a fine book without the presence of this imaginary dog, it is all the better for having him.

## Truth or fiction?

So, did the events of *Three Men in a Boat* actually happen? Jerome, in his introduction to the book, says that it is: 'A record of events that really happened. All that has been done is to colour them.' This should be taken with a pinch of salt. Montmorency, we know, did not exist as Jerome did not own a dog at the time. Carl Henschel, we also know, was teetotal so hardly worthy of Jerome's regular reflections on his lack of sobriety. The haunting incident where the group discover the body of a dead girl at Goring was borrowed from a local paper. It is likely that the book represents an exaggerated composite of some incidents that may have happened over the course of many pleasant river journeys. It certainly captures the spirit of such trips, and while Jerome's written geography is not always perfect, it is clear that he knows the river like the back of his hand.

Jerome boxed himself into a corner by making the trip a river one. Kingston to Oxford was fine, but how to make the book interesting when the journey downriver would cover the same locations as the journey upriver? Simple. He did this by finding an excuse to end the trip early – in this case in the rain at Pangbourne. While this solution is hardly subtle, it does its job of ending the book on a wry and reflective note admirably.

## The Illustrations

Little seems to be known about A. Frederics, illustrator of the initial editions of *Three Men in a Boat*. We do know that he was paid £10 for the sixty illustrations in the book, and was suggested by Jerome himself. His illustrations came in for some criticism amid the general tone of mild hostility towards the book, and despite the charm of many of them, it is not difficult to see why. There are two types of illustration in the book. Many are simple and slightly crude sketches illustrating the humourous incidents in the book. Some of these look like they took little more than seconds to produce. Other illustrations are more ornate and produced with greater care. A sketch of the mill and weir at Iffley, for instance, is nicely done, as are the ornate opening letters of each chapter, produced as a pastiche of medieval illustrated manuscripts. Overall, these illustrations act as worthy mood-enhancers, drawing the reader into the tone of the book, but as late editions have shown, it works perfectly well without them.

Examples of the two different styles of illustration used by Frederics: Uncle Podger (above) puts up a picture and the camping skiff in the rain (below).

## An overnight success

*Three Men in a Boat* was published on 3 September 1889. Its path from manuscript to print seems to have been a smooth one, as Jerome's discussions with his publisher J. W. Arrowsmith, reproduced in the annotated edition from the 1980s, suggest. There was some debate over royalty and Jerome asked for – and seems to have got – 7*d* per copy gross royalty on an edition retailing at 3*s* 6*d*, there having previously been some debate over whether to issue the book as a 1*s* or 3*s* 6*d* edition. Jerome also negotiated a rise to 8*d* after 10,000 copies had been sold.

Despite some poor reviews the book was a huge, and instant, success. 'One might have imagined – to read some of them – that the British Empire was in danger,' quipped Jerome, feeling, understandably, that as a humourist he was being sneered at. However, in a letter dated 20 January Arrowsmith confirms that he had printed another 7,000 copies, bringing the total run so far – this was a hardback that had only been out for four months, let us not forget – to 50,000. The US edition was published in April 1890 and sold very well. Jerome reckoned the US sales to have been over a million by the time he wrote *My Life and Times* in 1926.

By anyone's standards, his little tome did all right for him.

Jerome reads his reviews?

## *Three Men in a Boat* in Film, TV, the Stage and Radio

Given that the book is, supposedly at least, a travelogue with light relief rather than a novel with any sort of tangible plot, attempts to adapt it for other forms of media have been mixed. There have been three film versions plus a filmed adaptation for BBC television. The first two – a 1920s silent film starring writer actor H. Manning Hayes as Harris (and featuring transatlantic film star Florence Turner as 'Baby Twinkles') and a 1933 adaptation starring Billy Milton as J (in the film *Jimmy*) – are now difficult to track down. However, a glance at the credits and cast lists demonstrate that both films must have been somewhat free adaptations of the book.

The same can also be said of the better known 1956 movie, available on DVD, starring Laurence Harvey as George, David Tomlinson as J and Jimmy Edwards as Harris. While the adaptation does feature several of the set pieces from the book, usually featuring Edwards – Harris attempts to sing a comic song, Harris gets lost in Hampton Court maze – too often the film gets bogged down in slapstick and its wafer-thin plot. The characters of all three protagonists are adapted and accentuated to fit the story. J becomes an unsure recently-married man (probably a knowing reference to Jerome's own recent marriage at the time of writing the book), George a ladies' man looking to escape commitment and Harris a pompous buffoon. It's a harmless and fairly entertaining watch, but frustrating for fans of the book.

The most impressive version is the 1975 BBC TV film, adapted by Tom Stoppard (a fine choice) and directed by a young Stephen Frears, later to helm films as diverse as *Dangerous Liaisons* and *The Queen*. In the main roles are Tim Curry as J, Michael Palin as Harris and Stephen Moore as George. All three do well, although Curry's performance is a little sensitive for J and Palin just a touch broad. However, it is the adaptation's one-hour length that helps, allowing Stoppard to concentrate on many of the book's more episodic set pieces rather than getting tied down in unnecessary plotting.

At least two TV documentaries have sought to recreate the trip celebrated in the book. *Three More Men in a Boat*, which first aired in April 1983, featured journalist and radio presenter Benny Green, writer Christopher Matthew and lyricist Tim Rice, with narration from the book by Ian Charmichael. Green and Matthew also wrote the superb annotated edition of the book in 1982, later reissued to commemorate its centenary in 1989. In 2005, the trip was recreated once more, this time by three comedians, Dara O'Briain, Rory McGrath and Griff Rhys Jones, and shown over two one-hour episodes at the beginning of 2006. Again available on DVD, this formula has sparked several sequels (although yet to feature a cycling tour of Germany!) and for fans of the book, it is surprisingly satisfying. The three characters interact amiably, but with some of the sparky bickering that makes the book itself so enjoyable. The pitfalls of hiring a camping skiff – as real in 2005 as they would have been in the 1880s – are fully explored, as are many of the other themes, such a laziness, pomposity and the tendency to pack too much. Rhys Jones takes the role of the experienced father figure, O'Briain the amused everyman and McGrath the closest to one of the book's actual protagonists – 'fat and incapable' as Rhys Jones describes him. Harris, surely. Oh, and there's a dog called Loli. The opening titles declare that Jerome is turning in his grave. One genuinely suspects not.

There have been at least three different stage adaptations of the book, to this author's knowledge, two presented as one-man shows. The first, nominated for an Olivier Award in the early 80s, was by actor, writer and chairman of the Jerome K. Jerome Society Jeremy Nicholas. The second won the Stella Artois prize at the Edinburgh Festival in 1997, and was presented by *Likely Lads* actor Rodney Bewes. A production adapted by actor Clive Francis (and also featuring Simon Ward and Neil Stacey in its 2011 production – a bit old for the parts, chaps?) has toured periodically since the mid-2000s. A generation before any of these productions, another actor/writer, Hubert Gregg, became closely associated with the book, reading sections on more than one BBC radio variety programme. His autobiography includes an encounter with an incredulous Max Miller, amazed that a book reading should be on the same variety bill that he was topping, a performance for which one presumes he was paying his writers handsomely. Gregg, best known for his long running Radio 2 programme *Thanks for the Memory* and for writing the song *Maybe it's Because I'm a Londoner*, also contributed to the screenplay of the 1956 movie, and starred, alongside Kenneth Horne and Leslie Phillips, in a musical radio version first broadcast in 1962.

Given the nature of the book, it lends itself brilliantly to being read and performed rather than adapted into something else. Versions of the book, either in abridged or non-abridged versions, can be obtained read by Ian Charmichael, Hubert Gregg, Hugh Laurie, Martin Jarvis, Anton Rogers, Steven Crossley, Nigel Planer, Frederick Davidson and Charles Collingwood. The online audio book seller Audible.co.uk also offers two different unabridged versions in Italian (*Tre uomini in barca*) and one in Swedish (*Tre man i en bok*). Some of these adaptations pander to the popular cliché of Englishness – certainly the Charmichael and Laurie versions fall into that bracket. We know that the three protagonists represent a sort of newly affluent lower-middle class, rather than the upper classes so beloved of cliché. However, the choice of Laurie to read a two-hour abridged version, given his TV casting as P. G. Wodehouse's Bertie Wooster and Oxbridge background, suggests otherwise. During the planning of this book, my constant inspiration was the nigh-on perfect Martin Jarvis audio book. Unlike Laurie's version, which is somewhat hesitantly read in an abridgement that concentrates on the journey rather than the off-topic diversions, Jarvis' version is performed with huge affection for the source text. Whichever version you choose, please pick an unabridged adaptation, or you will lose the richness of Jerome's wondrous diversions.

# The Thames of Jerome K. Jerome

*Three Men in a Boat* was written at the beginning of the Thames leisure boom. Though the starting point for their trip – and this section of this book – was Kingston, in *My Life and Times* Jerome states that more often they would get the train to Richmond. He also mentions that later – one presumes he means after the 1880s – the river became too crowded, and that they usually began their trips at Maidenhead.

At the major towns along the route there would still have been considerable hustle and bustle, yet the developments, both commercial and residential, that pepper the riverside today would not have existed to anything like the extent that they do now, and between settlements like Kingston, Maidenhead and Reading the river must have felt remarkably peaceful, particularly when Jerome first began his exploration of the river in his 20s. Even though one cannot imagine cows paddling opposite Hampton Church, as shown on page 31, there is a sense of peace in many places along the Thames Path even today. Ironically, at the larger towns like Reading the river would certainly have been dirtier than it is today, and it is hard to imagine the discovery of a dead dog floating on its surface anywhere along its stretch, as J, George and Harris discover when they attempt to make tea from river water.

The Thames at its most alluring, at Goring in the spring.

There have been a few other changes. Maidenhead is no longer the pleasure hub it was in the Victorian era, when London society made its way en masse to this otherwise non-descript Berkshire town at the weekend and Boulters Lock found itself cited in dozens of divorce cases. On Ascot Sunday in 1888, 800 boats passed through the Thames' busiest lock. On the sunny weekday afternoon in mid-June that I photographed the lock, I saw one boat pass through in 20 minutes.

Elsewhere, particularly as the river narrows further upriver, many of the settlements remain largely as they once were. The only difference is the presence of the motor car. While villages like Clifton Hampden and Datchet feel blighted by their closeness to busy roads, despite their beauty, other villages like Iffley, which retains a delightfully remote character despite its closeness to central Oxford, and, further down, Goring-on-Thames seem to have survived largely unmolested by time. On a sunny day, at certain vantage points, it is not difficult to transport oneself back to Victorian England for a moment.

Although my family has a long association with the Thames, we have spent most of our time either in the Shepperton/Weybridge area or closer to Central London. It was something of a surprise for me to realise how beautiful the river around Goring and Pangbourne is. It is as breathtaking now as it must have been in Jerome's time. Indeed, with the completion of the Thames Path, which runs all the way from the river's source near Cricklade to the Thames Barrier in London, conditions have never been better to take in the best of what the river has to offer.

The following pages, which comprise the majority of this book, give a flavour of the river between Kingston and Oxford. Although Jerome will have known parts of the river closer to London as well (indeed, an incident at Kew Bridge is referred to in the book), I felt that as this is a companion to *Three Men in Boat* specifically, we should trace the progress of the journey as J, Harris and George did. *Three Men in a Boat* does not end at Oxford. The travellers turned around and finally abandoned their journey in the rain at Pangbourne and the book itself finishes at an unnamed restaurant in Central London.

The majority of the new photographs were taken by the author in two bursts in the spring and early summer of 2012. A few others have been borrowed from other photographers (with permission). These are interspersed with period photographs, mainly from the 1880s and 1890s, to provide some contrast between the river as it is now and as it would have been in Jerome's time. Once in a while, as with the pictures of the memorials at Runnymede, for instance, there are points of interest that Jerome could not have seen. In the main, however, even in the new millennium, this is still Jerome's river. Enjoy the journey.

## A brief note on locks and weirs

A lock, should any reader not be aware, is a man-made chamber which allows a water craft to navigate a waterway that is not on flat terrain. It does this by artificially moving the craft from one level to another. Almost all locks do this by 'locking' water in a chamber at one level, then letting water out or in until the level required is reached to let the vessel out again from the other side of the lock. This is what is known as a 'pound' lock. There are many variations on this theme, but most locks follow the pattern shown below, at Shepperton.

Weirs are barriers across the river, like sophisticated dams, which allow artificial control of water. A weir allows water to pool above the structure and flow over the top to varying degrees. They can be used for permanent water control when needed, particularly around locks, or to control water on a temporary basis, for instance as a way to control flooding. A weir is shown in 'action' below.

## The River Thames – a very brief history

The River Thames is German. 30 million years ago, before Britain ceased to be part of mainland Europe, the Thames was a mere tributary of the Rhine. The Thames developed its present course during the last Ice Age, and by 3,000 years ago had settled into its current, meandering course. Over the centuries its 177-mile course has seen hundreds of different settlements, from the growth of London to the smallest villages and farms. History has been made on its banks and islands, including the signing of the Magna Carta in 1215. As the Port of London became the largest port in the world in the seventeenth century, the Thames became vital for the dispersal of those goods. Reading, for instance, received 95 per cent of its good via the river.

In the eighteenth century, management of the river had been taken on by the Thames Navigation Commission, but competition from the railways in the early part of the nineteenth century led to a steep decline in commercial river usage. In 1866, the Thames Conservancy, which had previously only managed the Thames from Staines downriver, took control of the entire waterway from Cricklade to Yantlet Creek. The new conservancy set about improving the state of many of the locks on the river, whose toll income had often ceased to meet maintenance charges. Provision was also made to nationalise weirs and the 1866 act also prevented new flows of sewage into the river, the closure of existing sewage works that did so, and the control of the water companies operating on the river.

Most importantly, with the changing times, the Thames Preservation Act was passed in 1885 to enshrine the preservation of river for leisure. It prohibited shooting on the river, which had become a cause of concern. The act noted: 'It is lawful for all persons for pleasure or profit to travel or to loiter upon any and every part or the river' (apart from private cuts). The act also extended registration, already applied to the dreaded steam launch, to all pleasure boats.

Since 1974, management of the river has jumped around rather, passing firstly to the Thames Water Authority, and then upon privatization to the National Rivers Authority and then in 1996 to the Environment Agency, which manages the river now.

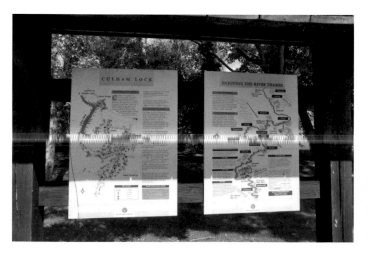

One of many very useful signs up and down the Thames, usually to be found at locks, which give visitors a flavour of the history of the river.

# Jerome's Thames
# from Kingston to Oxford

# KINGSTON

Kingston was just one of several options available as starting points to Londoners wanting a holiday or simply a day out on the Thames. Jerome describes some of the back streets as they come down to the river as 'quaint', and while Kingston does still have the odd quaint street, they are a fair way from the river itself. Nonetheless, for a large town, the developers have been reasonably kind to Kingston's riverside as these two views from the Bridge show, one from the early 1900s and the other from the present day

555  KINGSTON-ON-THAMES. — *The Bridge.* — LL.

There has been a bridge at Kingston since the medieval era which contributed considerably to the town's success as a market town. Until Putney Bridge was built in 1729, it was the only bridge between Staines Bridge and London Bridge. The first stone of the current bridge, designed in a simple, elegant, classical style, was laid in November 1825. Plans to erect an iron bridge had been abandoned due to the rising cost associated with the project. The old photograph, taken around 1906, is shot from the Middlesex bank, and the view beyond the bridge is now dominated by the John Lewis department store. The new photograph is taken from the Surrey side. Both feature public transport – an Edwardian tram and a twenty-first-century bus.

Jerome is reported to have been a friend of Richard Turk, who ran R. J. Turk & Sons, the oldest boatyard on the river and still there today. To hire a camping skiff for the trip would have cost them £3 15s. To buy one outright would have cost £30. It is here that the three protagonists who recreated the trip for the BBC in 2005 started. Other customers of the boatyard included Queen Victoria and Count Tolstoy. The elegant wooden-clad building remains, though it now looks incongruous among the modern buildings along the river front. Also shown is one of the other boat builders in Kingston around Jerome's time, Alf Burgoine.

# HAMPTON COURT AND MOLESEY

Hampton Court's main role in the book is to provide one of its best-loved sequences, Harris' inability to find his way to the centre of, and then out of, the maze at Hampton Court followed by an increasingly angry crowd of visitors. The maze, alongside the formal gardens, remains one of its best known attractions, and was probably planted during the time of William and Mary. The first picture here shows the Maze as it looked just after Jerome's time. Those in the picture look a little happier to be in the Maze than those in the second, which is one of Frederics' original illustrations from *Three Men in a Boat*.

Next we have a couple more views of the area, the first the Palace as it is now and the second the bridge itself. Then, as now, the Palace was one of Britain's most popular tourist attractions, having been built by Cardinal Wolsey for Henry VIII in 1525. Although expensive to get into now, if you have never been it is well worth a visit. The bridge itself links the palace on the Middlesex bank with Molesey on the Surrey side.

*Hampton Court Bridge*

It is typical of this remarkable river that a few hundred yards beyond the bridge the river takes on a feeling of genuine peace. Molesey (spelt Moulsey in Jerome's time) has a lock that was one of the busiest on the Thames. Less so now, of course, but it is still an attractive lock and the houseboats on the walk towards Hampton are varied and unusual.

# HAMPTON

Hampton Village itself is again used by Jerome as a jumping off point for a set piece, this satirising the fad for looking at tombs and old churchyards, something that Harris was very keen on. Hampton Church (pictured) still houses the ornate tomb of Mrs Susannah Thomas, only daughter of the governor of the Africa Company Settlements, the object of Harris' interest. Also buried at St Mary's are the celebrated eighteenth-century tenor John Beard and David Garrick, nephew of the famous actor.

The strangely amusing picture above shows the church from across the river with a herd of cows seemingly paddling. A ferry service runs between the two banks here. Below is a sight that the three companions could not possibly have seen. This beautifully-maintained houseboat is called *Astoria* and was originally commissioned by impresario Fred Karno, who wanted a boat that could house a ninety-piece orchestra on deck. It is now owned by rock guitarist David Gilmour, who has refitted it as a recording studio. He recorded the last two Pink Floyd albums there and his 2006 solo album, *On an Island*.

# KEMPTON PARK, SUNBURY AND WALTON

At Kempton Park, Harris and J stop for lunch and have an altercation with 'a gentleman in shirt sleeves' who accuses them of trespassing. Now, the area is best known for its racecourse (above). The other features dominating the Kempton Park bank of the river are the reservoirs that first began supplying London with water in 1897 (below).

The quaint Lower Sunbury village makes the best of its river locations, with tree-lined landscaped gardens looking over the water.

From Walton up to Shepperton, the Thames takes on a pleasant homogeneity. This is the Thames as middle class, commuter belt housing estate. Yet it still retains its beauty, and the contrast in housing, from neo-classical mansion to attractive flat developments to wooden cabin, provides plenty to look at. Walton is described by Jerome as 'rather a large place for a riverside town' where 'only the tiniest of it comes down to the water'. This is pretty much true today, and the river passes Walton at the very busy road bridge. The bridge itself is currently being replaced, and should open in 2013, making the area something of a building site! Above we see Walton Marina, one of several in this well-to-do part of the Thames and below we see a Thames path sign with some typical development for this part of the river on the other bank.

## SHEPPERTON AND WEYBRIDGE

The river becomes quite complex at Weybridge and Shepperton, which lie on opposite banks to each other, since three other waterways all enter the Thames at this point: the River Wey, which runs down to Guildford; the Basingstoke Canal; and the Bourne (two small rivers with the same name that meet at St George's College, Weybridge). The Wey enters the river in the photograph above. Below we see the footbridge that leads to D'Oly Carte Island, previously owned by the impresario who produced Gilbert and Sullivan's light operas.

Across Shepperton Lock is Hamhaugh Island, one of the largest residential islands on the Thames. Access is either via the river or across a narrow weir. The author and family spent many happy years at Cygnets, the bungalow owned by the Civil Service Rowing Club, which has views across to Weybridge. The island was created as a result of the weirs and the lock, which helped solved the shallowing of the river at this point, unpopular with barge owners. In Jerome's time the site – as with the rest of the island – was used for camping, and Cygnets was established in 1909 (above). Gradually over the years the island has been developed for housing and now has forty-six properties. This photograph (below) taken from the air shows the beginnings of development.

Two views of Shepperton Lock, one of the most attractive and well-visited locks on the Thames, above in mid-summer and below, unusually for this or any other book about the Thames, in mid-winter. It was here that Harris and J picked up George.

# STAINES-ON-THAMES AND CHERTSEY

The town of Staines changed its name to the rather more evocative Staines-upon-Thames on 20 May 2012, a move which won the town some short-lived national publicity. The change was to promote the town as a riverside location and thus boost the local economy. The river around Staines Bridge is well developed, with attractively-designed offices and flats on either end of the bridge, but the area also boasts The Hythe, a charming and unspoilt community. Above we see The Hythe from the nineteenth-century bridge, and below we look back towards the bridge from one of the pubs in the community.

Chertsey (as Jerome might say) is an ancient and pleasant town. It has an elegant eighteenth-century bridge, one of the more important ones on this part of the Thames as, despite the sleepy nature of the town itself, it is close to the M25, London's orbital motorway. Above we see the bridge from the nearby lock, and below the lock itself.

# RUNNYMEDE

Runnymede is, of course, the location of the signing of the Magna Carta on 19 June 1215. Jerome describes the events in ornate and fanciful detail. It is not difficult to imagine the book full of such descriptions, and we should be eternally thankful that it is not. However, as a one-off, this section is not without its charm. Magna Carta island now houses a pleasant, privately owned house, glimpsed through the trees in the delightful old photograph above. For J, Harris and George, however, that would have been it for this stretch of the river. For us, there are now three memorials to visit within a few moments' walk of each other. 188 acres of the meads that are now owned by the National Trust were donated by Lady Fairhaven to commemorate her husband. The two lodges (one now houses a tea shop) were also erected for the same purpose in 1929, and are shown below.

The other two monuments are the Magna Carta memorial, erected by the American Bar association in 1957, and the Kennedy Memorial, dedicated to President John F. Kennedy.

# DATCHET

Datchet is a charming little village somewhat blighted at peak times of the day by traffic caused by a railway crossing. This will be a regular theme as we work our way through this section of the book: pleasant villages fighting to maintain their identity against the motor car. In *Three Men in a Boat* Datchet becomes an eventful overnight stop for the three, as they attempt to find somewhere to stay. The two inns mentioned, the Manor House and the Stag, are still in business. The Manor is now a chain hotel while the Stag is much more a 'local'.

# WINDSOR

The town of Windsor does not feature particularly in Three Men in a Boat, but is worth a brief mention here. The picture above is what Jerome and friends would have seen as they rowed past. This area of the river has developed considerably over the years. Above Eton, at Boveney, is the Olympic rowing course. Below is Boveney as it would have been in Jerome's time – a view of the quaint lock in the 1890s.

Above is a view of the river at Windsor from the bridge between the town and Eton and below we see Bells of Ouseley at Old Windsor, one of the pubs mentioned in *Three Men in a Boat* and described as 'picturesque'. Well, today it is a busy Harvester, but the river views are still lovely.

# BRAY

A tiny village in Jerome's time, we'll pause a moment at Bray for a couple of modern-day reasons. Firstly, Bray studios is here, best known for being where the Hammer films from the 1960s and 1970s were made; it is still a working film and TV studio today and impossible to photograph, as the author discovered. However, the village itself has become synonymous with food, and houses two 3-star Michelin restaurants, Heston Blumenthal's 'Fat Duck' (shown on the right hand side of the road above) and Alain Roux's 'Waterside Inn' (below).

## BOULTERS LOCK AND MAIDENHEAD

Clearly, Jerome was not a fan of Maidenhead. 'Too snobby to be pleasant, it is the haunt of river swell and his overdressed female companion.' It is also fair to say that things have changed in the past 100 or so years. In Jerome's time, Maidenhead had something of a reputation as a weekend haunt for the London smart set, keeping the divorce courts busy! Boulters Lock, perhaps the best known on the river, was often the focus point of this activity. Ascot weekend was its highpoint of the year, and on Ascot Sunday in 1888, 800 boats passed through the lock. On a quiet Tuesday in June, the author saw one in 20 minutes (pictured).

Two more views of the lock. The first is of the lock itself as it is now, and the second is the recently-refurbished Boulters Hotel, which sits snugly behind the lock itself. Ray Mill Island can also be found beyond the lock.

10609. - THE BRIDGES FROM BELOW MAIDENHEAD.

Two older views of the river at Maidenhead. The town has a long river frontage. Note the Eel traps on the footbridge in the picture below.

## CLIVEDEN REACH AND COOKHAM

Cliveden Reach is the first genuinely picturesque stretch of river west of London, and is much drawn, painted and photographed. A couple of good examples are shown above and below. Just after Jerome wrote *Three Men in a Boat* the Duke of Westminster sold the estate to William Waldorf Astor, who lived at Cliveden House in great style, and continued to reside there after making Cliveden over to the National Trust in 1952. Stephen Ward introduced Christine Keeler to John Profumo at Cliveden in the summer of 1961, so it has its place in history as well.

Two more views of Cliveden, the top is from the first edition of *Three Men in a Boat* by the illustrator A. Frederics, one of a number of more ornate drawings in the book, while the bottom photograph is by the author from Cookham Bridge.

The village of Cookham itself is charming, with an unspoilt high street, and was the home to artist Stanley Spencer. The Stanley Spencer Gallery houses a permanent exhibition of his works. Kenneth Graham wrote *The Wind in the Willows* at Cookham Dene. The river here acts as a boundary between Berkshire and Buckinghamshire, and its Iron Bridge (shown below) dates from 1867. The picture of the attractive Ferry Hotel (above) was taken from the same bridge. Brunel was considered for the project to build the bridge but was rejected as he was too expensive.

# MARLOW

After his dismissal of Maidenhead, Jerome has only good things to say about Marlow. 'Marlow is one of the pleasantest river centres I know of. It is a bustling, lively little town.' Jerome is right. Marlow retains a huge amount of charm, and its river frontage is stunning, dominated by the beautifully maintained suspension bridge and All Saints Church on the town side of the river. The stay in Marlow is an eventful one: as well as their comic resupply episode, Montmorency has a chastening episode with a local cat. In these two pictures we see the approach to the river with the war memorial and church in the background (above), then the church again photographed from the suspension bridge (below).

Marlow Bridge is the only suspension bridge on the non-tidal part of the Thames and was designed by William Tierney Clark. It was built between 1829 and 1832. Above we see this glorious bridge in all its splendour and below a lovely view from the bridge itself.

The party put up at The Crown while in Marlow, and it is here that the group restocked, giving us a tantalising glimpse of social history in the sorts of retailers they would have visited, and how they would have received their goods. Jerome here describes the procession and below two pictures of modern day Marlow can be seen.

Montmorency, carrying a stick.
Two disreputable-looking curs, friends of Montmorency's.
George, carrying coats and rugs, and smoking a short pipe.
Harris, trying to walk with easy grace, while carrying
a bulged-out Gladstone bag in one hand and
a bottle of lime-juice in the other.
Greengrocer's boy and baker's boy, with baskets.
Boots from the hotel, carrying hamper.
Confectioner's boy, with basket.
Grocer's boy, with basket.
Long-haired dog.
Cheesemonger's boy, with basket.
Odd man carrying a bag.
Bosom companion of odd man, with his hands
in his pockets, smoking a short clay.
Fruiterer's boy, with basket.
Myself, carrying three hats and a pair of boots,
and trying to look as if I didn't know it.
Six small boys, and four stray dogs.

# HENLEY

The week and a bit that the three friends spent on the river was just before the Henley regatta. We know this because Jerome refers to it when he and George spend an evening in Henley while Harris has the – possibly imagined – incident with the swans. However, Henley plays such a major part in the history of the river one way or the other that it is worth lingering here for a few pages. The river is wide here and Henley Reach provides a magnificent natural course for rowing. We begin in relative tranquillity with two views of Henley outside the regatta. Above, we see the bridge with the Angel Hotel beyond. Below shows the Reach devoid of pleasure or rowing craft, except a sailing boat in the far distance.

A couple of contemporary pictures of Henley; above is the entrance to the wonderful River and Rowing Museum at Henley, beautifully situated by the river, while below is the view of the river that can be seen from the museum.

*Marsh Lock, Henley-on-Thames.*

Two more old views of Henley: above, Marsh Lock just above Henley; and below, a typical view of house boats. Before the Thames Preservation Act of 1885 it was quite normal for a poor property owner to find a houseboat dumped in front of their properties, particularly during the regatta. The Act made this more difficult.

*House-boats at Henley.*
*2617.*

Henley Regatta. Even today, Henley remains the most prestigious regatta of the season – rowing's equivalent of Royal Ascot. Henley was the original location of the University Boat Race between Oxford and Cambridge in 1829. In 1839 the annual regatta first took place. Originally universities and public schools took part, but in the modern era Henley is also a place for rowing clubs. The author's 15-year-old niece, Ellen, coxed a crew from Walton Rowing club in 2012. These first two pictures give an impression of how the regatta would have been in Jerome's time. Above, we see the course during a race. Note the huge number of pleasure craft to either side of the race. The picture below shows the craft closing in as the crews complete the race.

In the final picture (above) we see the chaos created by the pleasure craft of Jerome's time. The scene seems completely chaotic and unregulated. It is a wonder any races were run at all! In the picture below we fast-forward to the 1980s, almost exactly 100 years after Jerome's time. We see Temple Island, starting point on the Henley Course, but also note the dress of the people on the bank to the right. The boaters and blazers that were the fashion in Jerome's time remain in fashion at Henley, as a tribute to a bygone era, an era that *Three Men in a Boat* has done much to perpetuate.

Two more shots from the late 1980s. Both show the contrast between the old and the new. The brightly-dressed revellers in the punt (above) contrast with the bare-chested spectator to the left, while the rowing boats below contrast with the distant marquees that mark the modern, commercial regatta of the modern era.

## WARGRAVE

The river is pleasant enough at Wargrave, but Jerome does remark, in one of his 'travelogue' moments, about the sign of the George and Dragon Pub. One side – showing George killing the dragon – was painted by George Leslie and the other side by his friend Mr Hodgson – which shows George enjoying a pint afterwards. Both signs remain (above) and the pub itself is shown

## SHIPLAKE.

Shiplake has significance in *Three Men in a Boat* as the place that the party moored when George and J visited Henley. It is here that Harris was supposedly accosted by swans, and also here that the whisky bottle supposedly went missing. The river itself is lovely here, very similar to how it would have looked in Jerome's time (above). Below we see swans at Shiplake. Descendants of Harris' attackers, perhaps?

## SONNING

Jerome also has a great deal of admiration for the village of Sonning: '... the most fairy-like nook on the whole river. It is more like a stage village than one built of bricks and mortar.' The village retains plenty of hints of that now, although like many of the villages in this book it has become a slave to the motor car attempting to cross the wonderful red brick bridge. The current structure dates back to 1775, and has been much painted over the years. Above is a view with the Great House Hotel prominently visible beyond, while the contemporary photograph (below) shows a similar view with the hotel now hidden by vegetation.

Jerome recommends the Bull Inn at Sonning (above), and it was here that the 2005 BBC party stayed. Sonning Lock had the reputation as one of the prettiest on the river, and the lock keeper is clearly very proud of his floral creations, as he poses in front of the lock in this colourised picture.

## READING AND CAVERSHAM

Jerome has little good to say about 1880s Reading, resorting to its historical significance as the trio pass through, although it looks pleasant enough in the photograph above. Nor is the river at its finest here in the twenty-first century, but once again development could have been far worse, and down towards Caversham it improves further (below).

Two more views of the river at Caversham, the top showing boat houses in the distance, rather than the commercial development that can be seen looking towards Reading Town, and (below) the decent concrete bridge built in 1926.

## MAPLEDURHAM

Somewhat off the beaten track by road, the Elizabethan Mapledurham House and working mill present a charming view from the river. The house, owned by the Blount family, is seen in the picture above, just beyond St Margaret's Church. The watermill (below) is the only working mill on the Thames and dates from the fifteenth century.

## PANGBOURNE AND WHITCHURCH

Continuing upstream, this is a simply stunning part of the river. Jerome mentions Pangbourne only briefly on their journey towards Oxford, but the village takes on added significance in that it is the place that the travellers ended their journey on the way home. We begin this section with two views of the river at Pangbourne.

The Swan Inn is mentioned in *Three Men in a Boat*, and it remains there still, proudly displaying its sixteenth-century origins and its stunning river setting (above). In Jerome's time it had a boatyard, and it was here that the party left their rain-sodden craft on the way home. The view below may well have been their last view of the Thames on that trip, minus the iron posts one suspects!

And so to Pangbourne Station itself. Today the station combines remoteness with the modern trappings of railway travel. Despite those trappings, one can still imagine J, Harris and George waiting on the London-bound platform, fantasising about warmth and a decent meal in the capital.

Whitchurch, on the other side of the river, is only accessible for motorists via a toll bridge. This gives it a secluded, exclusive feel. The old toll house itself is shown above, and the details of the tolls as they would have been in 1792 are also shown. These days, only cars and lorries are charged and the new toll booth is shown below. Cars cost 40p, and vehicles above 3.5 tonnes are charged £3.

Two views of the ironwork bridge that joins Pangbourne and Whitchurch, taken from the latter village. It was designed by Joseph Morris and built in 1902.

## GORING AND STREATLEY

Goring is another important stopping off point for Jerome. As well as staying here for several days in the story, there is also the incident – beautifully placed by Jerome as the only serious moment in an otherwise joyful book – when the party find a dead body of a young girl in the river. Frederic's drawing for the book (above) references Millais' famous painting *Death of Ophelia*. In fact, while the story behind the death is true, Jerome did not discover the body, but lifted it from *The Berkshire Chronicle*. Below is a view of the villages from a nearby hill.

The three lunch at The Bull (above), though it is not recorded where they actually stayed – presumably the same inn. The superbly located Swan is not mentioned in the book, although it is discussed extensively by Michael Palin in his *Python Years* diaries. The crew and cast of the 1975 Stoppard adaptation stayed at the Swan and Palin was not a fan, although he does refer to it as one of the most beautifully located hotels in England. Looking at recent reviews of the hotel, it seems to have improved in the intervening 37 years!

The twin villages of Goring and Streatley – like Pangbourne, Streatley is in Berkshire, like Whitchurch Goring is in Oxfordshire – straddle the Thames in delightful fashion. For someone most used to the pleasant but relatively built-up and homogenised river in Surrey and Middlesex, visiting these two charming villages was a revelation. Above is a view of the stunning houseboat moored next to the Swan hotel and below is a view of one of the weirs next to the bridge that connects the villages.

Two more views of the Thames at Goring. Jerome refers to the area as strong for fishing, as it remains, and uses this as a jumping off point for a typically wry and funny dissection of the exaggeration of the typical angler.

Above and below, two views of the delightfully-located Goring Lock and overleaf, another stunning view of the Thames at Streatley.

# WALLINGFORD

The Thames kisses Wallingford pleasantly at the medieval bridge which links the Oxfordshire town with the village of Crowmarsh Gifford. The town itself has much to offer, and the town centre is dominated by its Corn Exchange, now used as a theatre (above), and St Mary-Le-More church (below).

Two views of the Thames at Wallingford from the bridge

# DORCHESTER

The river passes within half a mile of the historic settlement of Dorchester, now a sleepy village with some nice country hotels, but once an important town. First settled in Neolithic times, it later became an important Roman settlement and then a Saxon town. For a while it was the Episcopal centre of Wessex, and later had an Augustinian monastery until the dissolution in the 1530s. Until the creation of its bypass, its place on the main routes from Gloucester and Oxford to London made it an important stopping-off point for travellers. Above and below show how lovely the village remains.

A colourised view of Dorchester from the river (above) and (below) the relatively nondescript Days Lock, which Jerome offers as a decent stopping off point from which to see the village.

# CLIFTON HAMPDEN

Jerome recommends the lovely village of Clifton Hampden, which he describes as 'a wonderfully pretty village, old fashioned, peaceful and dainty'. It retains much of that character today, despite the cars queuing to cross the bridge at peak times. Above is a view of the church from the 1890s and below is a contemporary photograph of buildings in the village. To my eyes, it retains more of that picture-postcard quality than Sonning, although this is very much a subjective view!

Jerome does, in particular, recommend the quaint pub The Barley Mow, and although it no longer rents rooms it is still an excellent place for a meal and a drink. Its ceilings, Jerome adds, would not suit the heroine of a 'modern novel' who is always 'divinely tall' and always 'drawing herself up to her full height', thus smacking her head on a beam.

# CULHAM

Culham has some interest for Thames-aficionados as its lock exists in a 'cut' – an artificial channel created in 1809 alongside a new lock which replaced the original pound lock, which was unpopular with bargemen as its tolls were expensive and the lock itself difficult to navigate. The new section, however, cut nearby village Sutton Courtnay off from the trade that the Thames brought as the river no longer flowed directly past. The hilliness of the area between here and Oxford makes this the deepest lock on the Thames. Above we see the road bridge photographed from the lock, and below the cut itself with the lock in the distance.

# ABINGDON

Abingdon. From Below.

As Jerome points out, Abingdon has one of the more interesting river frontages in that the streets of the town come down to the riverside, as are shown in these two photographs from different parts of the town and from very different eras show.

When the author visited Abingdon in April 2012, the rowing club was holding its Spring Head, a local regatta. A shot of locals walking to the regatta site can be seen below, taken from the bridge, while above we see rather more stylish revellers at a similar event from shortly after Jerome's time.

Above we see the plain but impressive fifteenth-century bridge at Abingdon. Below we see the painting that represents the family tree of one W. Lee, who died in 1637. The tree shows that Mr Lee, who was five times mayor of Abingdon, had 197 descendants, leading to a comment from Jerome that he hopes there are not more of his kind in 'this overcrowded nineteenth Century'. The painting can still be found in St Helen's Church.

# IFFLEY

Visiting this sleepy little village, it is almost impossible to believe that it is little more than a mile from central Oxford. The lock and weir itself are charming and feel very remote. When Jerome and friends would have passed through, there was a working mill at Iffley, but it suffered a disastrous fire in 1908. The burned-out remains are shown above. Now only the weir remains here, shown below with the lock in the distance.

On this page we see two views of the charming lock itself. The original lock was one of the first 'three pound' locks on the Thames, built before 1632. The current version of the lock was built in 1923.

## OXFORD

We end the journey with a few pages celebrating the river as it arrives at Oxford. The Thames (or Isis as it is also known at Oxford) does not flow through the centre of Oxford, but several hundred yards to the south of the city at Folly Bridge. The famous boat builders Salter's operated from both sides of the bridge, and above we see a lifeboat being launched around 1900. The boat building side of the business no longer operates, and this building is now the Head of the River, a popular pub (below).

Old and new views of the Thames at Folly Bridge. The bridge was erected in between 1825 and 1827 and was designed by Ebenezer Perry of London.

Looking back over the Isis from Folly Bridge. Salter's pleasure boats remain prominent today.

COLLEGE BARGES, OXFORD.                                                                    1 12.

The main difference between the river scene now compared to how it would have been in Jerome's time is the absence of the rather grand college barges (above). These have now been replaced in rather less ornate fashion by boat houses (below). We finish our trip up the Thames with this final photograph of Folly Bridge from behind (next page).

# Index